Juvenile

SCHAUMBURG TOWNSHIP DISTRICT LIBRARY

1257 01470 0933

Schaumburg Township District Library

130 South Roselle Road

Schaumburg, Illinois 60193

The ELVES and the SHOEMAKER

The **ELVES** and the

SHOEMAKER

Retold and Illustrated by

PAUL GALDONE

Based on Lucy Crane's translation
from the German of the Brothers Grimm

CLARION BOOKS
NEW YORK

SCHAUMBURG TOWNSHIP DISTRICT LIBRARY
JUVENILE DEPT.
130 SOUTH ROSELLE ROAD
SCHAUMBURG, ILLINOIS · 60193

3 1257 01470 0933

398.2094
CARMANY
GALDONE, P

To Americo Loiola, master shoemaker,
and family

Clarion Books
a Houghton Mifflin Company imprint
215 Park Avenue South, New York, NY 10003
Copyright © 1984 by Paul Galdone

All rights reserved.
For information about permission to reproduce
selections from this book, write to Permissions,
Houghton Mifflin Company, 215 Park Avenue South, New York, NY 10003
Printed in the USA

Library of Congress Cataloging in Publication Data
Galdone, Paul.
    The elves and the shoemaker.
    Summary: When the poor shoemaker and his wife
discover the two naked little elves who have helped them
become successful, they sew fine outfits for them.
    [1. Fairy tales. 2. Folklore—Germany] I. Title.
PZ8.G127E 1984   398.2′1′0943   [E]   83-14979
RNF ISBN 0-89919-226-2   PA ISBN 0-89919-422-2

WOZ 20 19 18 17 16 15 14

There once was a shoemaker who, through no fault of his own, became so poor that at last he had nothing left but just enough leather to make one pair of shoes. He cut out the shoes at night, so he could set to work on them the next morning.

Because he had a good conscience, the shoemaker laid
himself down in his bed and fell asleep at once.

In the morning, after he had said his prayers, the shoemaker went to his workshop. There he found the pair of shoes made and finished, and standing on his table. He was very much astonished, and could not tell what to think.

He took the shoes in his hand to examine them more carefully. They were so well made that every stitch was in the right place, just as if they had come from the hand of a master-workman.

Soon a customer entered, and as the shoes fitted him very well, he paid more than the usual price for them.

Now the shoemaker had enough money to buy leather for two more pairs of shoes. He cut them out at night and intended to set to work the next morning with fresh spirit. But that was not to be, for when he got up they were already finished.

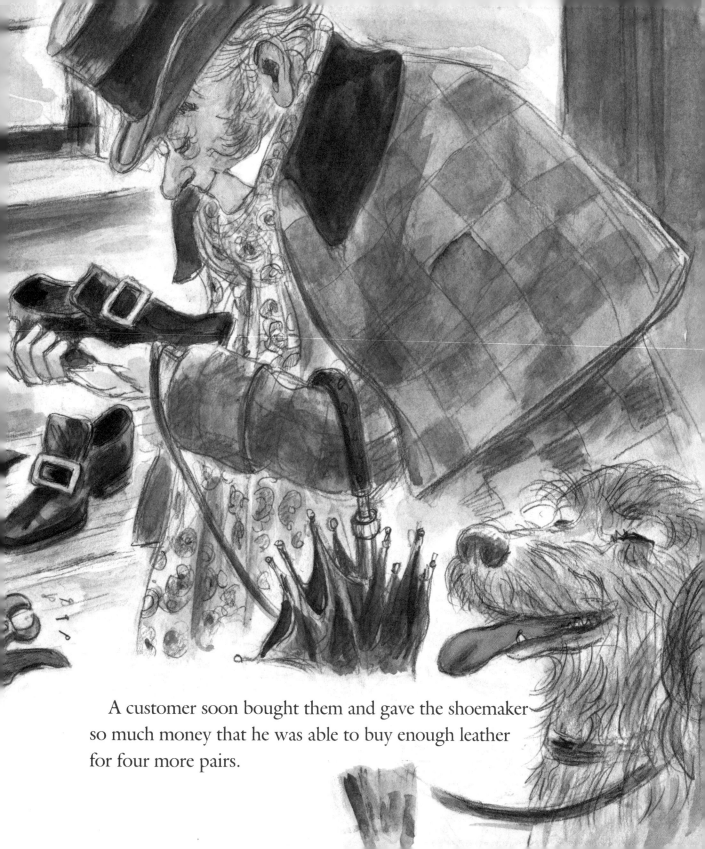

A customer soon bought them and gave the shoemaker
so much money that he was able to buy enough leather
for four more pairs.

Early the next morning he found the four pairs finished also. And so it always happened. Whatever the
shoemaker cut out in the evening was finished by the
morning, and soon he was making a very good living.

One night, not long before Christmas, when the shoemaker had finished cutting out the shoes from the leather, he turned to his wife before he went to bed and said: "How would it be if we were to stay up tonight and see who it is that does us this service?"

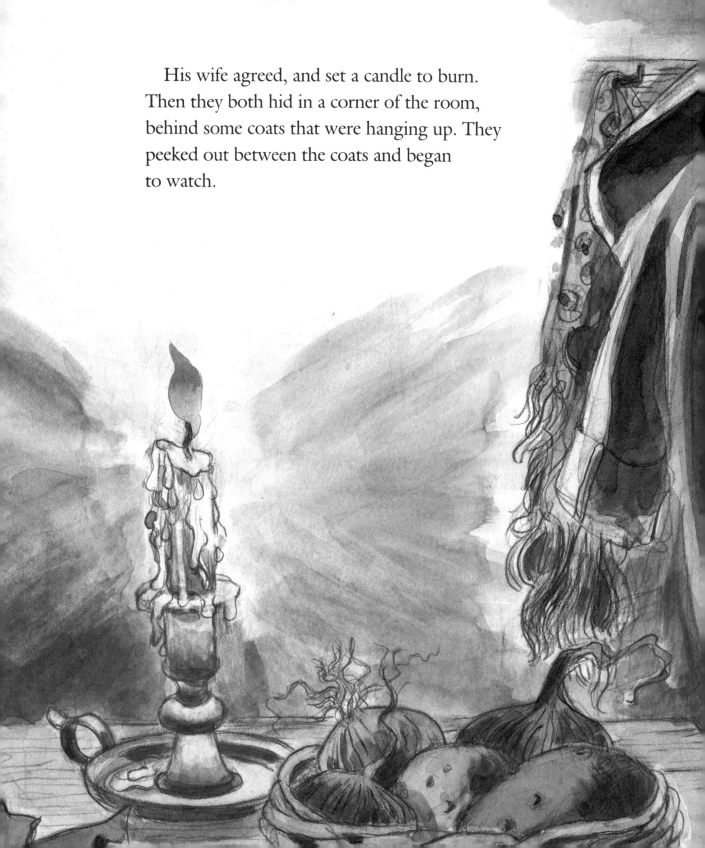

His wife agreed, and set a candle to burn. Then they both hid in a corner of the room, behind some coats that were hanging up. They peeked out between the coats and began to watch.

As soon as it was midnight, in came two
neatly-formed naked little elves. They seated
themselves on the shoemaker's table, took
up the work that was already prepared,

and began to stitch, pierce, and hammer the leather.
The elves worked so cleverly and quickly with their
little fingers that the shoemaker's eyes could
scarcely follow them, so full of wonder was he.

The elves never stopped until all the shoes were finished and were standing ready on the table. Then they jumped up and ran off.

The next morning the shoemaker's wife said to
her husband, "Those elves have made us rich,
and we ought to show them how grateful we are.

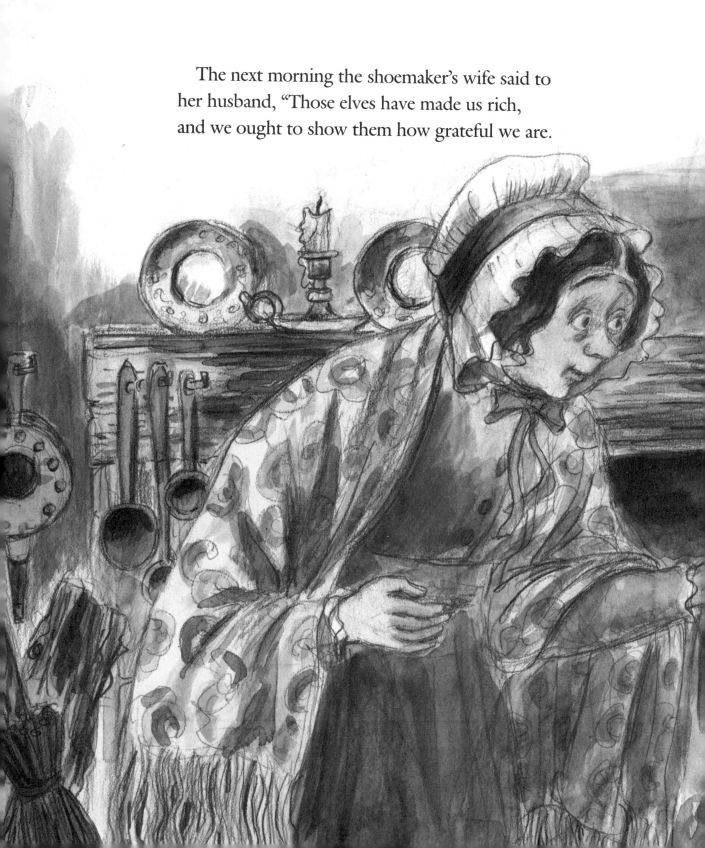

With all their running about, and nothing to cover them, they must be very cold."

She smiled. "I tell you what. I will make little shirts, coats, waistcoats, and breeches for them, and knit each of them a pair of stockings. And you shall make each of them a pair of shoes!"

The husband consented willingly, and that night,
when everything was finished,
they laid the gifts on the table
instead of the cut-out leather.

Then they hid themselves so that they could observe
how the elves behaved when they saw their presents.

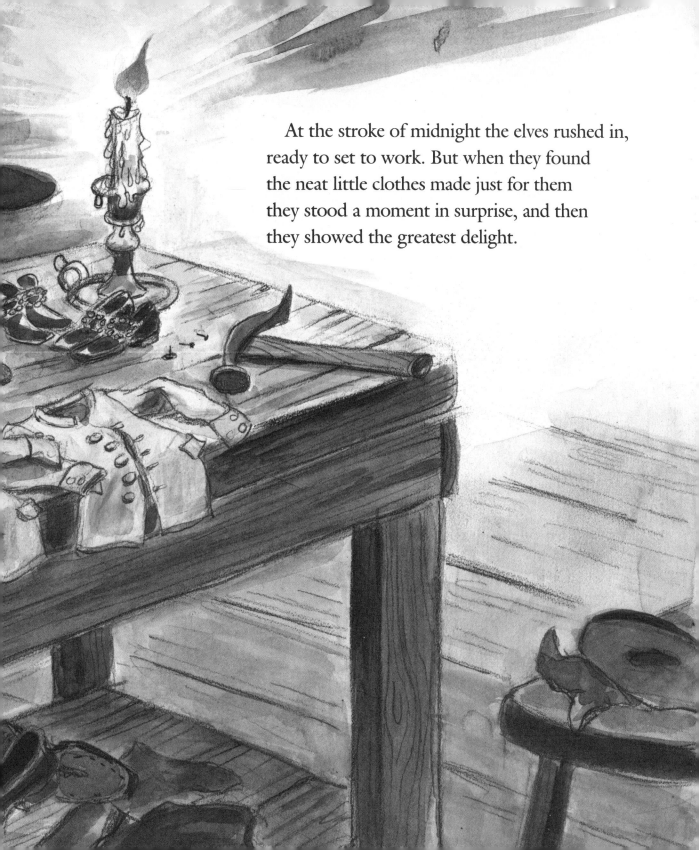

At the stroke of midnight the elves rushed in, ready to set to work. But when they found the neat little clothes made just for them they stood a moment in surprise, and then they showed the greatest delight.

Quickly they took up the pretty garments and slipped them on, singing,

What spruce and dandy boys are we!
No longer cobblers will we be.

They hopped and danced about, jumping over
the chairs and tables, and at last they danced
out the door.

From that time on the elves were never seen again.
But the shoemaker and his wife prospered as long
as they lived.

4767015